Cereremonials

Katharine Coldiron

KERNPUNKT • PRESS

Art: Cover "Magia" and interior illustrations by Mariana Magaña de Lio
Book Design: Jesi Buell

1st Printing: 2020

ISBN-13 978-1-7323251-5-9

KERNPUNKT Press

Hamilton, New York 13346

www.kernpunktpress.com

for Florence
and
for Violette

I

Concentrate, you said.

I can't. I'm asleep.

Open your eyes, you said. *No, keep the lids closed. The inside eyes. Like a black pool clearing.*

You are not my Corisande.

Look for the tree curving over the gravestones, you said. *That is me. And the cool grass. And the mist clinging to the ground. That is me.*

I'm asleep.

Find me standing, you said. *My dress is pearl and my hair is black glass. That is me. I'm waiting for you. Concentrate. Concentrate.*

Are you my Corisande?

I am a shade, you said. *That is me.*

In the wardrobe is the white dress for tomorrow. I slide it over my head. The Directress will be angry. The window is open, the breeze swaying in, curtains not quite flapping. Fluttering. Like breaths, like your breaths. *That is me*, you said. The curtains are not lace, they are organdy. My white dress, for tomorrow, flutters with your breath and mine.

Outside is the blessing of night air, the kiss of it. *That is me*, you said. *Concentrate.* The girls all sleep inside like cicadas under the earth. Tomorrow they will chatter in the trees. The curtains flutter. The hem of my dress brushes the ankle-deep grass, tiny knives on the insteps of my feet until I run far enough from the school, from the sleep of the earthbound girls, that mist clings to the ground and makes the grass soft. Soft, cool, like fur growing on the animal earth. *That is me*, you said.

A great tree curves over the gravestones. Moonlight, as alive as a candle flame, silvers all with the same elegant light.

Where is my Corisande?

Concentrate, you said. Your voice is a piccolo. I know it is you. I feel your heart as if it's my own.

I cannot contain it and I dance. I spin like a top on the grass softened by your mist, arms fingertipped together over my curls and twirl and twirl and cartwheel and cartwheel and the piccolo trills me to a halt: *Concentrate.*

I fall. My heart slows to match yours again. Joy is mine; sobriety yours. You were always the responsible one. Even now my white dress, for tomorrow, is wrinkling under my weight and the grass has smeared some of its bright tone—exuberance is mine—on the crinoline. The Directress will be angry. She will think *Corisande would never have appeared for Baccalaureate in such a state* but she will check herself, because I am still mourning, still unstable from the loss. She will not say it.

Where is my Corisande?

My dress is a pearl and my hair is black glass, you said. *Find me standing.*

I have lifted my white dress for you. The Directress will be angry. My eyes close. I teethe my lip. My Corisande. Your voice. My Corisande.

Open your eyes, you said. *Like a black pool clearing.*

And there you are, standing, glimmering, outlined in golden thread, your skin rosy as a peach. I cannot stand so I crawl, hard knees staining my white dress, I crawl and I clutch at your calves and I crack open my heart to howl at the tree that curves over the gravestones, you, glimmering, the thing in my arms a flat stone carved with your name, Corisande, and the dates of your life, which ended last week in a lake a half-mile from the Cartwright School for Young Ladies, you, glimmering, your black hair floating like moss in the water, in the air, your dress a wet pearl. *Concentrate,* you said.

You are not my Corisande.

You are not my Corisande.

II

I wait there all night long.

The graveyard is quiet but life abounds. The tree alone, in the wind, has twenty-five sounds. The grass is secretive. No one sees me, not until the blackest strip of night, when I am alone, when I am alone, as convinced of alone as I was convinced of quiet when your head fell from your hair under the lake for the last time, unsplashing.

The sky does not lighten. It grays. There is such a difference. One glance and the sky is blackblackblack, the next and it's gray. Not turning the lights on; trying out a new color swatch against the existing dress. One color, then another, distinct. The shades are arbitrary.

Then you—not you, but the you I've retained under my hair—whisper to me. You tell me to go back to school, to try and rinse out the grass stains on my white dress (for today), before it's time or they miss me. The Corisande I tasted last night is gone with the blackblackblack. I had her for a night. That is enough, the inner you tells me. Patience. There may be another night. You are still counseling me, still and ever.

Now the sky lightens, pouring its darkness down and away, ink diluted in a cool bath. The wind freshens, awakening like a secret, sneaking out of bed and down the hall before the rest of its family. Heat escapes in my breath. Step after step I draw back to the school, slumberous and benign and scattered with shadows. Night hasn't cleared off completely. The birds are cautious yet. It's so many hours before Baccalaureate starts. The grass stains are just smears on my dress in the nonlight, the gray. I could peel them off like dried glue.

The hallway is windless. I tiptoe, but the boards do not sleep or wake with us and they make noise as heedless as it is when girlnoise covers it. Clap my hands on my ears—if I don't hear it, it isn't—and you giggle at the folly.

Letty pops her sleepyhead out of the room she shares with Carol the Great. "Amelia," she breathes. My name is a snake uncoiling when it's whispered. (In your mouth it was heliotrope curling over a garden wall.)

"Shh."

"What are you doing?"

"I have to fix my dress."

Scraping sleep breath behind the door. Letty has been kind to keep it to herself if Carol the Great snores nightly.

"Let me help."

"Nooo, go back inside." Your spell, your golden thread, is on the dress. No one can touch it.

She tiptoes in the warm spots my feet have made. "My poem woke me up. I've been lying in bed saying it to myself."

"Aren't you doing Frost?"

"Two roads diverged in a yellow wood. And sorry I could not travel both. And be one traveler, long I stood."

"Do you like that poem?" The wood spoke to us, but the bathroom tile is chilly and mute.

"No. It's my mother's favorite. She's coming up to hear it."

I close my eyes.

"I'll go to the kitchen for bleach." She steals out. The sink drips.

Emptier without Letty, even though I didn't want her. Her eyes full, steady, always. Now I am alone with you and the lack of you.

I shed the white dress. Crinkle and rustle. It cannot

lie flat on the tile. Music brushes the walls, too light to echo. The hot bath, your hands dipping the surface, music, music from the chapel, one hundred sisters singing. Rehearsing for God, before God. For today.

Letty comes back as the skin of my back is warming the floor, as I sport with the white dress and the memory of your hands. "Amelia," and the voice is not yours. She does not drop the glass bottle but it is a near thing.

Letty's eyes know. "You miss her."

Yes. I clutch the dress.

"I met a boy last year at the ice cream social." The faucet gushes. Letty adds capfuls of yellow-clear acid. Spreads her fingers to keep them away. "Sometimes he's my pillow. He's what I hug. Or I kiss my arm, like my sister showed me." She demonstrates, romancing the inside of her elbow.

"What's his name?"

"Harvey."

Harvey whose name is Mudd. I press my smile into the dress.

"Bring it here. The water's hot."

The stains rub out. The bleach slips and slides across our fingers. Letty cups the solution and spills it across the fabric. She seems to know what to do. Her mother?

"How'd this happen?"

I went to the cemetery last night to see Corisande, I assemble, but no. You float over this moment too heavily as it is. "I don't know." Knees, crawling. "I must have worn it on a picnic."

Letty's silence forgives this flimsy, this clumsy wisp of a lie. The dress was new last week. I slipped it on and Corisande knelt, giving the balcony speech in her nightgown, the hallway's open doors and curious heads giggling. I fluttered a hand on my silk white bosom and flushed red, red.

Dawn outside the clouded glass. Nothing stirring yet, but. "Go back to bed. You shouldn't get in trouble."

Letty rinses her hands at the next sink, runs her clean finger down my wet braid. "Walk with me? To chapel?"

The stains are nearly gone. "Yes. Okay."

The hallway, creak by creak.

Wring the dress with towels, spread and blot and wring some more. The fruitless, pushing scent of bleach. Drip and sip of leaky faucet. Music brushes the walls. Faint. Come, gentle, black-browed night. The obsidian curtain of your hair. Shade my reddened fingers.

I, clean and dry, walk with Letty and Carol the Great

and Carol the Small and Irma. We form a line of white pickets: three pairs missing a sixth. So many others crowd my senses, grown people in thick clothing and resistant siblings cooped up half the day getting here. The bells drift under or over but not through the clutter.

The Directress is already inside, crisp and gray, tiger's-eye buttons down her front to catch more light. I am not presenting and I have no one in the guest pews, ribboned and bowed yesterday afternoon by the third-form girls. Irma stays with me in the side seats. She wants a gray mare for her birthday, so, in her elaborate system of kismet and bestowal, she doesn't mind being invisible to the ribboned pews. She speaks, but she is so dreadfully not you that she speaks in Russian and I shrug and half-smile because those are safe answering gestures to incomprehensible people. She stops speaking.

The organ opens its droning throat. The bells even more distant, though nearer. Through layers of stone. Girls drift in, sit whitely in the rows ahead. They do not speak. The organ filters note by note into the layers of rustle against my thighs, the pew vibrates, it's nearly time.

"We are here," whispers one to the other, in front of me.

Their skin shimmers. But no, none of them are you. None. Not one. (Irma and I, alone in our pew.)

The organ plumes its peacock feathers, iridesces the air in the peaky rafters. The choir stands. Black folders open. Irma fusses with buttons, cuffs. The girls in front of us glow with the voices, when they begin. They gleam. I see them and feel their cold rustle, their out-of-fashion skirts and embellished hats. Irma does not see. Still there is no you. The choir lifts, tippy-toe voices in the shimmering air. All the rustling girls are watching the processional in the main aisle.

It is you.

Dripping. Black seaweed hair. Stockings rumpled down. Squish, one strapped shoe, squish, the other. The choir dips and swoops up again, high as a sparrow, no lumbering prideful peacock. You, glimmering. Everyone faces forward, the choir; only the cool rustling girls in their hats watch the aisle. Squish. Your heart a fair sun, arising. No, no, you were Romeo. Squish.

Hovering beyond your shoulder a dim thing. Like a stain in the air, a patch of wall long covered with a portrait. You flick at it, a mosquito at your ear. Drops of lakewater cascade to the carpet. Glimmering.

The organ spreads its clawed feet, this time, buzzing

under our pews in the lower registers, and the choir clings to one last note. Next is the Alleluia. I can't see you when the whole church stands up, except I can. You dance. You are dancing. Agitated, hysterical, the way one dances with a bee in the garden, tossing your arms at the dim spot in the air. Surely they around you can feel the lakewater flying in all directions. Irma sings the Alleluia with verve and sass. Her knee pops in and out, rocks her body. Do you need me? Should I go? The Directress will see me. Will see my white picket dress. Me the odd fifth. She lost you, too, the Cartwright School lost you. It isn't only me. That is real, present, actual, sitting in my skull even as I wail and weep and insist that you were *my* Corisande, you belonged to no one else.

The Directress would have seen you. Through the Alleluia-faces you squirm, wet hair here, white arm there. The dim spot. The Directress sees me, not you, and I Alleluia instead. It's nearly done, this part, nearly on to the one-by-one, girl by girl behind the pulpit with her voice and her memory.

Everyone sits and you see me. Smile. (The dimness no longer there.) You dance now, instead, with the music in the bathroom, the stuff from the cup of my ear, a conch you hold to your own. What else but music between our skins?

The choir again. No organ. Just they—ave, ave, ave. Rising. Ascending. And you. Rising. Ascending. Feet toes down, heels drifting. Your eyes not on mine. The rustling girls half-lift, open to join the song. Wait. No. NonononoNO.

Up and run through, gasping, rising, muttering. Many hands. Many hands. Only you, only this—you, ascending. The gray severe Directress, her buttons flashing. No, no.

I catch at your heel. Barefoot summers made a rich callus; I never tickled you. It's just air, mist, on my fingers, but you look down. The Directress there, or near-there, her face too bright to rage. Her face a heart. She wants me to know (she said, the day after) that she feels for me, she understands how close I was to Corisande. She wants me to know (she said) that she knows it isn't going to be easy to get over. But life goes on. We, the living, must move forward. *While you molder alone,* I cry, under the skin. Alone.

I catch at your heel. Mist. You, glimmering. I cannot read your eyes, their darkness too complete. The choir. Ave, ave, ave. Not ascending.

All things pause, just once. Her bright face, her

sensible hand reaching out to me—not grabbing, to clasp—and the choir and the rotation of the earth that binds my feet (but not yours). All. And then the rustling, whispering, rustling girls rise and come into the aisle to put their hands on me. Like clouds passing, my skin the sky. *She is going,* they say to each other, to me. *We are here and she is going.*

"No," I say. Their hands on me. *Yes.*

Ave, ave, ave.

The Directress reaches me and pulls my hand out of the air and walks me back to the side seats, next to Irma, who is white to the eyebrows and sitting stiff. Her terror of the Directress stokes itself as I sit sandwiched between them, the Directress holding my left hand loosely in her right. "Nearly over," she says to me, whispers, to soothe, I think. I am not soothed. You ascend. The rustling girls lift their arms to push you off. Ave, ave, ave.

Then you look back. You look down at me. Your eyes hollow pools. Their fire has fled. You are no longer there. The you under my hair just dumb playback, me mixed with you to keep company; the you in the aisle equally incomplete, the sun's reflected light on an airless satellite. You are not my Corisande.

And you descend. You shrink and descend, the girls

murmuring, reaching out and touching their lips and telling each other these tidings, and you pass over all the assembly in ribboned rows and finery to me. To me. The Directress does not see you. Not you, but the bright glow you have become, the half-Corisande that remains after the lake drew you down. She hovers before me, glimmering, eyes and smile just off yours. *I am here*, you say. *I am here with you.*

Ave, ave, ave.

III

The last time we were together. The lake, yes. Do you want me to tell it like a story?

The other way would be to press it down in pictures. My hands on your head.

Yes, I like words better too. It's just slower. I don't know how much time we have.

Oh.

Yes, I'll begin. We went to the lake to let go, and that year we went nearly every week. Amelia insisted. I did not mind the Cartwright School, I even liked it, but Amelia had a funny mix of feelings about it. I think because she carried her mother's death like a burden, like a crown of shame. It was such a bright color to her, that shame, and she thought everyone else could see it as well as she could.

The lake. Yes. We went there to scream or laugh as loud as we wanted, no danger of demerits from the prefects for disturbing the peace. We went there to be alone together, to pretend no one else had ever seen us. We were Lewis and Clark on new ground, conquering and discovering, enclosed by wilderness but not lost. We had each other.

We swam in the lake, played games, told stories. And we loved each other, in that place where no one could see us.

I want to tell you how I loved Amelia. Is that all right?

I loved her like my best friend with sugar on top. That's as close as I can come. We had the same kind of bond Jane Eyre had with her Helen, only I've never sorted out who was who between us. Maybe no exact parallel exists. I was the louder, the more extroverted, and I was the one who died; but I always behaved myself and remained, like Jane, below the eye-line of those who could harm me. And like Jane, I had relatives who cared little for me, and I would come into money eventually.

I don't know where Amelia, neither feisty nor dull, fits in this imagining. She was ever my Juliet, though, my inexplicable, ineradicable object of desire. The friendship was Jane and Helen's with a passionate romance smoothed over it like icing. Or it was a heated love like Romeo and Juliet's with a deep friendship underneath. Not one or the other but both.

And how seriously can you take all this? We were girls, unshaped clay, thrown together in the same hot little dormitory room. A kiln for love or hate or what-have-you. I can only plead to you of the strength of my affection for Amelia, as you have seen evidence of the strength of hers. A bit fearful, really.

Yes. The lake.

That night felt different only because we were so near the end. We neither of us knew what would come when Baccalaureate ended, when, two months hence, Graduation came and went and everyone's parents came to pick them up and take them away. My aunt had told me two hundred times that I could not live with her any longer once I had an education. We had relied on others' kindnesses to keep ourselves during school holidays—I sometimes went with Carol the Great and her mess of brothers, and Amelia took up a half-dozen offers from different girls across the years—and now that we had nowhere to go for this final, grand holiday, the lake felt even more like a friend. The water was so quiet. So unlike the roar of the ocean (Carol the Great lived on Martha's Vineyard), the eternal violence of the surf. A lap and a cool darkness that beckoned like Amelia's eyes, like the interior of her curls. I swam in there.

That night we took a boat. Just like bloody Dreiser. An overturned canoe languished permanently in the ivy, and we dug it out and pushed it onto the water and stayed dry for a while. We loved each other, Amelia with desperation, I with tenderness.

We found a way to lie comfortably together in the canoe, looking at the stars, brushing away spider stowaways from the ivy. An hour wheeled by, maybe more. The thump of her heart vibrated the boat beneath us. It shook us both.

"Has the Directress ever asked to see you alone?"

Amelia opened her eyes. "In her office?" Yes. "When I first came. She brought me in, asked me about my mother."

"Me too," I said. "Did she close the door?"

"I don't remember. Wait—no. She didn't. Halfway

through I heard a girl shout 'Madam, I'm Adam!' I think it was the first time I heard a palindrome."

"But the door was open?"

"Yes. Must have been." Amelia—I love saying her name, even now—Amelia tugged her blouse across her body, which had sprouted gooseflesh. The water brushed the boat. "Naomi, I moan," she said. "There's another."

"She closed the door last week," I said. "She saw me alone and closed the door."

Amelia, still dopey with love, smiled. "You're flunking out of Cartwright, I guess."

"No."

"What, then?"

"She said I can't tell you."

"Then why bring it up?" She cuddled up to me, her breasts chilly under the blouse. "You're cold. You're always so cold."

"I want to see how long I can hold my breath," I said.

"Okay, go ahead." She giggled. "Bird rib. Salt an atlas."

I roused and unknotted my hair. She ran her fingers into the spill of it, and I shivered.

"Tell a ballet," Amelia whispered.

"I think that'll do," I said. "I'm going in."

"You were serious?" She fitted her arms into her blouse. "You're already so cold as it is. You'll catch your death."

"No. We'll run back so I can warm up."

"Hold your breath up here. I can time you."

"It's bracing." I dipped half a hand in the water. Yes; *bracing*. I took up my rough wool skirt and fastened it on.

"Are you mad?" Her dreaminess had faded altogether. "Run back to Cartwright soaking wet? Stay here with me, darling. I'll tell you some more palindromes. Daedalus: wine. Peninsula: dead."

"You're the one who's mad." I drew on my white blouse.

"Don't go in the water," she said, and caught my arm. Her fingers imprinted warmth into my skin. The blood beat a hearty tattoo against her wrist. All this I could feel, so sharp in the night. As if I'd never been awake. A dove mourned, back on shore; the lake smelled of old copper and undergrowth; my own hair blanketed my shoulderblades, black snow. Moonlight shone in Amelia's eyes.

"I just want to see," I said.

So I dove in. No—I didn't dive, I more fell. I held my

breath for fifteen seconds, then thirty. One dip at a time, increasing increments. Then a minute. Amelia pleaded with me again and again, come back in the boat, come back, Corisande, come back in.

"You'll freeze," she said.

I couldn't tell her no, and I couldn't tell her yes. "I'm going to the bottom."

"Oh, no," she said, hooking at my wet shirt with her fingertips. She trembled. "No, let's go back now. The moon's nearly down. You can't get all the way to the bottom."

"Yes, I can," I said. The dove again, the coo skipping off the water until it perched on my shoulder. "I can and I will."

"I didn't mean you couldn't do it. Corisande, come on. Get in the boat and let's go back to Cartwright."

"I will touch the bottom."

"O, stone, be not so," Amelia said, with the remnants of a smile.

"Don't fret, love," I said, and touched her cheek. "See you soon."

And I went beneath. I found the lake bottom and I dragged my fingers through the muck, gathering pebbles and stones and shells, and I filled my woolen pockets with them. I hovered. My arms rose. The canoe floated, a seed pod, slightly darker than all else around it. I could not see the moon.

It is entirely different here, underneath. Quiet. Sweet.

I know that Amelia came in after me. She found me by my hair, snagged it on her reaching fingers. Her arms proved stronger than the stones in my pockets.

I know that they took me away from her by force. That they laid me out on the grass and covered me with a gray blanket and had to drag her off shrieking.

I know that they buried me under the great oak tree and that my aunt came to see me laid in the ground. The Directress gave most of my things to Amelia before my aunt arrived.

I know that the water was very cold. Until, eventually, I was colder.

IV

When I was eleven, my aunt took me to the seaside with my two cousins, who were composed of pastry flour and margarine. I'd never seen anything as large as the sea before. Anything that dwarfed my life to a cracked nut. It was the first thing I ever loved.

I had read Hans Christian Andersen, and I knew "The Little Mermaid." I knew about people who lived beneath the waves, beautiful women with yearning hearts and greedy witches with no hearts at all. At eleven I'd grown too old to believe I could live down there with them, but I did not exactly disbelieve in them. It was possible, I thought, to dive under the water and hear mermaids singing. If only just possible.

My cousins sang an atonal duet of complaint from moment one, but I focused on the sea to drown them. Drown them out, I mean.

Crash and foam. Fold and fall. Pull and expire. The bubbles and the tiny sand creatures and the restlessness and the blue, so blue, multihued like the cool shimmers in mother-of-pearl.

Queenly. My lady ocean.

I flopped into her lap with more enthusiasm than skill or safety. Above the surface boiled the opposite of peace, children gulls waves hotdogs popcorn butter fried dough sizzle colored towels umbrellas people people people. Underneath, wadded ears, clouded eyes. Dim noise.

All the day this high and low, bobbing like an apple— out of the sea and into the sea. I nearly forgot about my cousins. My aunt hollered intermittently. The lady's murmur parched me, while the sun shone, benevolent until it burned my indoor skin.

When the air cooled and the breeze freshened, my aunt took up hollering and wasn't inclined to stop. The swells emptied of bathers. Without thinking I turned and paddled out, an inept puppy fleeing an attempt to housetrain it. Further I went. The seaside smells dispersed. I thought of ice cream, the tin ladle of water by my bed. The water pocketed cold. I paddled on and on, the waves fading to weak, inconsistent frequencies. Sparks of sound, like sequins, from the shore.

A mouthful of seawater. Cough and it's okay. But

what's down there, underneath? What can find my feet?

Dunk my head. Cough. It's okay. The shore seems farther away than before. I paddle, but it doesn't get any closer.

If I fall, will I sink forever?

Another mouthful, more. Cough, cough. Maybe this is not okay.

Paddle harder. Electric red in my mind. Paddle faster.

The shore is quiet. I can't distinguish human figures, just a colorful blur.

I will be asked to do this again. It comes from nowhere, but beats like a pulse.

Dunk, for longer. My fingers, pruned, wave around like leaves in a quickening breeze. Cough, cough, cough, more water. Eyes burn. Skin stings. *I'm helpless* is what's overtaking me, the sense of being dwarfed by something more powerful than I will ever be. Encircled in the ocean's arms, squeezing my chest until my heart bursts and the dim becomes black. Is that singing? Triton's children calling me down?

I will be asked to do this again.

No, it's a whistle. The squeeze is the grip of a Samaritan, a strong holidayer from the next county who saw my dark head go under one too many times and pulled me back, against the undertow, and delivered me unto my aunt, who put on a tremendous show, weeping and wailing over her darling Corrie as I spat up seawater and struggled to get off the cold sand, which abraded my indoor skin. Everyone held me down against the sand. I never found out the name of my rescuer.

I will be asked to do this again.

I have wondered, recently, whether the rescuer and the Directress are one. I have wondered whether there are any coincidences. I have wondered whether any child, any normal, untouched child, could be so bewitched by the sea as to ask for another trip to the seaside on the very same day she was nearly drowned in it, on the way back to her bed in the attic, while her cousins wrestled noiselessly over a bag of sweets. Is that child aware of her fate, distant as she is from it in circumstance, near as she is to it in element?

The ocean has no bottom. A lake is self-contained, no matter its size. My feet found a place to land.

I blinked and my schooling was over. The girls had all grown into their noses. Without you it all blurred together, the days lost and the months colored blue, violet, aubergine, indigo. Carol the Small met a boy (a son of her parents' friends) and dreamed most of her classes into doodles. Carol Schuyler-Harrison. Mrs. Walter Harrison. CSH. Shhh, her future told her.

Letty was kind to me, but distant, and I didn't understand until a moment in the lunch line when I brushed her arm with mine and my skin might have been a hundred degrees. She jerked away. The dress, and you, made her flinch. Soft as her heart was, she feared my love was catching, could jump like a flea and infect her with unnatural longings. Dear Letty. She gave what she had.

And then Graduation—so many loving mothers, their faces dripping; so many snapped photographs, triumphant smiles. No hint of the pain borne later by women in labor, their men gripped by drink, car crashes, polio, burial of hopes in the warm yielding earth. No, just daughters, showing their teeth to the sun. I stood away, watched the Directress circulate. She had no color save gray.

The wind swept through the Cartwright School and scattered us, leaves, across the sky. I went to a city and attempted to begin life without you. Found a room to sleep in, floorboards where I planted memories of you. Found fellow humans to tell me the time, to lend me a match, to summarize their families in quantities. One of five kids. Second wife. First grandchild. After my last baby. I told them I had a sister who died. I told them my mother was back home, across the river. I told them I didn't have a special fella in my life. Fall came. Winter.

My voice, I learned, is beautiful. I sang too loudly in the bath, and my landlady (stooped, ancient, hiding the loneliness of age beneath nosy, stony cantankerousness) told Robert about me. Robert, on the second floor, worked in an office that cast vocal shadows for the fame-endowed.

Vocal shadows sing and give speeches behind curtains while the famed speak into dead wires. There is nothing about them that is not secret. They cannot seek the podium. This suited me. My voice had not been of much use since your ears drank it up. So I lent it out, for a price, to a woman who had a high screeching thing in her mouth. A model, Miss Audra Rose, hired for speaking advertisements without auditioning. She rarely appeared live, on a stage, for any reason, but when she did, there I stood behind the curtain.

I did not miss the use of my voice.

Letty married Harvey whose name was Mudd. Carol the Small had a child, a girl, and I knew without guessing that she lessened her stature by not delivering a male. Baccalaureate came, went, came and went again. Ave Maria. Leaves blew across the sky.

Robert the casting agent introduced me to a spiderweb of fellow creatures of the deep: other vocal shadows, day doubles, secret wives, bastard children. I went to dim rooms with them and drank fiery potions and laughed at their jests. Their faces included the same mark as yours and mine: a dive, at some point, from belief that we would be missed. Who will mourn me, now that you are gone? Who will look in my room for me, if my rent is paid and Miss Audra Rose does not need her voice?

I made money. I bought food. I slept. I asked for a

match, for the time. I found nothing pushing me from behind, nothing ahead that I wanted. You were the one with plans, with ambitions. I sought only to follow. I found myself at a trailhead, perplexed by freedom.

Again and again I ventured out for a magazine or a sandwich and found myself on my knees, on the sidewalk, surrounded by shoes and coat hems. I chased my own footsteps back to my bed. Breaking down, breaking down. A car with a shoddy alternator.

More and more, when I couldn't sleep or eat, I visited bars on the ground floor of the city. The more stairs I had to descend to get inside, the better.

One night, in a speakeasy nineteen steps down from the street and draped in shadows like me, I met Renate. Her hair wasn't stylish; it was bound up in old-fashioned knots fastened to the base of her skull. Her eyebrows arched like spider-legs above bright blue agates. The eyes, colored like yours, were how I ended up in Renate's bed that night, her hair unbound, so like yours that I tangled up my fingers in it mid-dream and, moaning, pulled her out of the phantom water. She fell on me with even greater passion while I wept in the dark. Ever and always pulling your heartless weight into the boat. Finding my way home in the wee hours, I crawled. Breaking down.

Renate and I barely communicated. Comings and goings, mostly, my place or hers, is there enough gin, what time do you need to get up. Renate wasn't a shadow like me, she worked as a clothes model for a couturier, anonymous in plain sight.

One morning, "My mother's coming to town next week," she told me. I shut my eyes. The illusion of you around her eyes and in her hair cracking to slivers. You do not have a mother. We are motherless children.

"Sorry. I can see you the week after."

Her shame didn't offend me. No one's mother goes to speakeasies, mates with shadow-creatures.

Carol the Great did not marry anyone. She did not become anyone's mother. She got into a car with three college boys and they raped her, all of them, and dumped her at a quarry outside of town. The fall fractured her skull and no one found her for a day or so (this was Saturday night, one of so many Saturday nights in small towns with fast boys in jalopies) and she was never right after that. Her hands built crooked crafts of thread and wood instead of embroidering flowers on heirloom linen; her mouth could only mumble. She sat alone in a facility for four years and then had a seizure and died, and again, no one found her for a day or so.

It's supposed to be the orphans who slip through the cracks.

VI

I saw Renate again the week after her mother left, at a penthouse party I'd already agreed to attend. Renate glided and I slunk along in her wake, using the voice I no longer owned as little as possible. I met Bettina that night, when she spilled a cocktail on me and I, heedless, took off my taffeta dress mid-party and ran it into the bathroom for baking soda and blotting. Bettina followed me and kissed my shoulder in that tiny powder room and then it was nights at Bettina's apartment, dodging Bettina's roommates, listening to Bettina's patter about her skirt-chasing boss while I ignored the tap of Renate's long, ghostly fingernails on the back of my neck. She could not possibly miss me. No one would miss me.

Bettina was such a contrast to you (blond, hazel-eyed, slumped and thin, unintelligent) that her face relieved me. Her whole interest in me came from experimentation, though, a gathering of ammunition for some interpersonal conflict. She'd also dallied with an undertaker's assistant named Cleo, and one night she asked Cleo to bring some cocaine over for a bit of fun. An hour in, Bettina's skirt-chasing boss arrived (he was even greasier, even shorter, even hairier than she'd allowed; more goat than man) and they went into the bedroom and closed the door. Sliding antes from player to player, lover to lover. So Cleo and I left together.

My mind raced. Cleo wore heavy Hollywood makeup but I sensed a shadow in her, a less-than which bound us.

"Where did the cocaine come from?" I asked.

She drove like a demon. The engine growled and leapt. She grinned, her hands easy on the wheel. "From Malcolm. Let's go see him."

"Can't we go to your place?" I didn't want to share Cleo with a man.

"His place. It's better."

I did not ask what that meant. Soon enough, I didn't need to. It was a bar, his place, a swallowing cave of green and black that obtruded its darkness upon the street. THE LABYRINTH in silver letters.

"Come on, Amelia." Cleo slung her arm around my neck.

No one knows I'm here. No one knows I'm anywhere.

The light shimmied and snaked about. The walls seemed to crawl with vines and serpents. The patrons were all children to my eyes, golden-haired youths and girls with mute faces, stranded in green leather booths in their sparkling clothes. I caught Cleo's hand, certain I'd lose my way in this place. Jazz moaned from somewhere, a saxophone and a trumpet with many mouths lamenting the world's sins, trading bar for bar and sin for sin.

"*Here* she is."

I thought the voice came from the figure behind the bar, but on this, surely, my senses were mistaken. Furred. Horned. Patches of brown and white covered his snout, his neck, tapering to his chest and shoulders. His impressive torso was bare. A silver ring gleamed under his wet black nose.

"Amelia, meet the Bull." This was so entirely what I expected to hear that I glanced at Cleo in alarm. When I looked back over the bar again, the Bull was just a tall, broad, enthralling human male.

"They call me that cuz I'm stubborn," said the Bull. His hand gripped mine like warm steel. The Directress's hand on my shoulder. "And other reasons."

"I knew you'd like him," Cleo breathed into my ear. A hot, spicy fragrance drifted near and I raised my hand to my nose. Stopped short of licking the fingers the Bull had touched.

"Malcolm," he said. "It's really Malcolm, my name."

"I don't like men," I said, quietly, to Cleo.

"You like this one. You're sweating."

A warm room. A warm night. Cleo's hand rested on the back of my neck.

"Why don't I meet you ladies in the back?" The Bull threw a bottle of bitters in the air and caught it behind his back.

"Let's dance," I said to Cleo.

"No."

"C'mon, one dance." I needed to get close to her. Remind my body of the shape of a woman, the heat of her. The ring in the Bull's nose kept catching the light.

"Have a dance, Cleo," said the Bull. "I'll tell them to kick it up."

She leaned toward me, toward him. "Yeah, okay," she said. The band, wherever it was, swung uptime. The Bull hadn't moved. Pairs of girls and boys emerged from the booths and tottered out to dance, overbalancing this way and that, sinking into the shadows off the floor and hauling their partners back again. Cleo's hair brushed cool, her cheek warm. She jitterbugged and I kept up, barely. I kept following her instead of myself and getting lost. The dancers' eyes rang hollow, and I never saw the band.

The back room, later, was odd: dark but golden. Mirrors with veins of fool's gold marring, or gilding, what they reflected. Clean, but shadowed. Like the Bull himself, who sat in a velvet chair and ran his finger around the rim of a martini glass of viper-green liquid.

"What have you brought me, Cleo? Is she sour or sweet?"

I dug half-moons into the meat of my palms. Sour. "She didn't bring me to you. I came here." I blinked and smoke streamed from his black nostrils, his curved horns dipped in gold. The Bull grinned.

"She's an amiable sort," said Cleo. "Met her at Bettina's. She asked about your candy."

"Nothing sweeter than that."

Sweat collected in the grooves of me.

"Try one of these." He offered his martini glass.

"Isn't this yours?"

"Now it's yours."

"The candy," said Cleo.

"Yes, I remember." He threw her a glass vial and she caught it near her face. The drink was based in absinthe, but it contained flavors and additions unknown to me.

I'd never seen a man with a ring through his nose.

"It keeps a leash on me," said the Bull. Had I spoken? Cleo opened the vial. I wanted to pet the Bull's fur. His grin dripped. My body cooled and heated again, perspiration and ventilation and the cool sliver of licorice on my tongue. My dress suddenly too long.

"You sing, don't you?" said Malcolm.

"How did you know that?"

"I can see music in a person's eyes," he replied. Cleo in the background tap-tap-tapping the vial out on the coffee table.

"That's absurd," I said.

He tilted his head down. "Is that really what you think?"

I looked away.

"Sing something for me," he said.

I half-laughed. "What, now?"

"Is there any other time?" Cleo sniffs and gasps, behind, exhales victory.

"No accompaniment?"

"You can hear the band from here." His ears twitched. "It's 'I'm Putting All My Eggs in One Basket.' You know that one, don't you?"

I did. Most of what I knew was minor-key, but I

liked Irving Berlin enough to know his cheerful songs, too.

"I can hear you better in here, without the band. Sing."

"No."

He scraped one foot across the carpet and exhaled noisily. "I told you I was stubborn. Don't tell me you're stubborn, too."

I could hardly decide which sandwich I wanted at the automat.

"Good," he said. "Then don't refuse me. Sing."

"Sing for 'im, Amy," said Cleo, dancing her way over. "We'll never get out of this room until you do."

"Music has charms to soothe the savage beast," he said.

"It's breast," I said. "Most people misquote it."

The Bull did not reply. Did not move. Cleo motioned impatiently. By habit I did not use my voice for myself, and by preference I didn't sing in front of strangers. But I wanted to be finished with this room and the clotted black eyes on me.

So I sang.

My voice echoed upon the mirrors. Cleo clapped

when I finished, and I felt rosy despite myself. I drank most of the green drink.

Malcolm clapped more slowly, still appraising me. "That hit the spot," he said. He patted his knee. "Come over here, Amelia."

Did I tell you my name?

"Come sit with me."

I laughed. "I'm not a child. I don't sit on laps anymore." The gold in the room gleamed brighter. Cleo's face stretched and dimmed, its makeup thickening along the sides. Her body lost focus, her form growing fuzzy.

"Never fear. You're not a child to me."

Was there something in my drink?

"No, no. I'm a gentleman."

It's the atmosphere. The temperature. What lies between thee and me.

"Come here. I won't bite."

Yes, you will.

Cleo hummed the band's tune, fading to the edge of the room.

Yes, I think you will.

VII

One early morning I come back to my own bed from Malcolm's and I find Corisande lying there, looking at the drawn windowshade.

I haven't seen you, I tell her.

Have you missed me?

Yes.

You radiate, she says. Something is doing you good.

It doesn't begin in the bedroom. He leads me through the swinging door inside the dim back wall, into an area built like backstage, hanging ropes and crates and stacks of textiles and empty bottles in bins. He leads me up a spiral staircase. His feet clonk on the serrated metal as if they are smaller, tougher than shoes.

I look at the windowshade, too. My window has no view of interest in daylight, but by night a field of colored stars overlie the menial geography of buildings and streets.

Why are you still here?

It's she who asks me, but the question does not belong to her alone. I asked it of her a moment before she asked it of me. As if I conjured her words. My questions are more specific than *still here*: Why does she stay in this coil? Why is she still a girl when fingers of age pluck at my bones and skin? Is there another place she ought to be when I find her in my bedroom in darkness, in my kitchen in sunlight?

Why haven't you come back to Cartwright? she asks.

He leads me across a catwalk toward a black box, ten by ten by twenty, suspended in the gloom and fog above the Labyrinth's floor. I peek down and there's the bar, there are the booths, there are the girls in black dresses circling with their trays. Their heads look vegetal, sprouting with fluff like pollen. The walls distant and smoky, undulous, indefinite.

I like the city, I say. I like my job.

There's no family here, she says.

That's true anywhere. I have no family anywhere.

You have me.

We're going in circles, I say, and unbutton my dress. Unroll my stockings. Unravel my hair. I did it up after Malcolm had made me sweat. The walk back, cool air on my neck, dissipated the heat but not the sensation.

You are unfaithful, she says. You have been unfaithful

to me.

She says it or I make her say it and I don't know which it is. I don't know what lies in my bed tonight, where it sits on the spectrum between what I invent and what I perceive, but she turns over and I see her bright blue eyes, beacons in a storm of bedsheets, and she is as real there as she was when I dragged her out of the water six years ago.

That's the bund, he says. He is behind me now, his breath hot, pressing. I bring them up here to play. No one knows where they are.

How can we hear them? I ask. Because I can. Music sinuous as the walls, just like the first night I came here. His voice is nearer, but not louder.

Holes in the floor, he says. One of his arms is draped around my neck. His fingers push under my dress. Hot hands. I don't stop him.

Isn't that dangerous?

They're small holes, he says. The other hand traces down my waist, into the crease above my left thigh. My dress too long, again. They're just there to release the sound. You couldn't even step through one.

I've never lied, I say.

Lies of omission are lies, she says. No fury. You have

lain with a man.

I'm not sure this is true, but Malcolm is not female, and this is her point. So I arrange shame on my features. I'm not what I thought, I tell her. I'm not what I used to be.

He has seduced you. Her fingers, dewy and strange, stroke my cheek, my freed hair. I understand, she says. The world is wide. I just needed to hear it from you.

In the past month I have begun singing at the Labyrinth. The past week, choosing my songs. Last night, I sang "My Man," and Malcolm told me couples filled the dark alleys outside, driven to consummate the desire in my voice. It's not a romantic song. It's not a song I'd ever sing for Corisande. It's about blind, stupid devotion to a personality that the song fails to define. Only as *my* man. That's all he is.

What I know about Malcolm is mostly empty space. But he is my man, and I sang to him last night, thickening the air in the alleys with my lust, like a red cloud, and now I can't tell Corisande any of it, her face on my pillow, her shape ill-defined but her eyes never clearer. I sang, my sweat and moan liquefying into the melody, to the girls and boys in the Labyrinth, but here she is (here you are) and there's nothing in my throat. My great love, the only one who mattered, and I can only think of the elbow of a musical phrase I sang, twice, "my ma-an...he's my ma-an..."

I want to see, I say.

Not yet.

I reach my own hand back. Now?

No.

We move like the walls. The music sways and catches above the dancers.

The sun is coming up, I say.

I'm not afraid of daylight, she says.

He didn't seduce me.

She doesn't say anything, so I say it again: He didn't seduce me. I wanted him, and I had him.

You wanted him instead of me?

I want you to sing for me, he says. Our hands roam, clothes pushed aside, but I haven't turned to face him. I don't know what will face me. The horns, or not.

I'll sing, I say.

Here, at the Labyrinth.

Any night.

I want you to stand up here in my cage and sing. To me. To no one but me. I want them to hear you, to hear your voice coming down, and I want them to know what I've done to you.

You haven't done anything to me, I say, my breath nearly gone.

Of course not, I say.

Obsession doesn't share like an obedient child, she says. It's greedy, but it's single-minded. There's room only for one idol at a time.

I love you, I say. I'm not obsessed with you. I'm not obsessed with the Bull, either.

She sits up. The bedclothes pass through her. He's a bull?

The real answer: In the dark, sometimes, it's impossible to tell. His power, his voice, the tang of his sweat and his hair on my palms. I blink sometimes and see his gold horns, his whiteless eyes. No, I say, it's his nickname. A joke.

It's not a joke, she says, mirroring me again. Bulls are dangerous. Untameable.

He crushes me, lifts me, kneels with me, fucks me. On the catwalk over the Labyrinth. He clamps a hand over my mouth. I afire, my knees bruising, my flesh stinging. He heedless, braying, grunting. Present and not vaporous. Whole and solid and me yielding around him, under him. Glorying. Blinking through the diamond shapes of the metal catwalk at the dancers below, lifting their heads at his commotion. Gasping. The band moaning low.

I'm not trying to tame him, I say. Has this entire conversation been me contradicting her?

Would you stop if I asked you to?

No. It slips out like a secret.

There's no place for me between you and him, she says after a long moment.

You're not between us. There's you and then there's everyone else. The Bull is everyone else.

Stop calling him that, says Corisande. It frightens me.

Me too, I want to say, but fright is not the beginning and end of the Bull to me. Thrills. Pain and tenderness. Emptiness beyond restoration when he leaves my body, fullness beyond capacity when he enters it.

That is the first night. The catwalk, and the band in its elevated cage. He also makes me yield, makes me scream, in his dark bed, in the alley, behind the bar (I do things that would shame you, my eyes filmed red with need), against the wall of the band's cage after they've vanished with their instruments and their dames. There is nothing he doesn't ask of me, and nothing I am unwilling to do.

You're my love, I tell her. I wake and sleep with you in my head and my heart. But you aren't really here. This isn't where you live. There's a space in the bed.

The chips of bright sea embedded in your face darken. It's not a space you have to fill, you say to me. And I am really here. I'm here because of you. I was ascending and you caught me. Don't forget. It's you.

Your eyes so dark now. Not a kind sea.

I don't even see you go, you're so dim. The sheets are just

missing you, of a sudden.

Where is my Corisande.

Come back to the Labyrinth.

It's dawn. The Labyrinth is so much a place of the night that I'm not certain it exists after the sun rises.

You won't sleep today.

Will I ever sleep again? If my Corisande is really gone?

Sleep is for the dead. Meet my body with yours.

Ah. My own lust calling. I am so used to Corisande under my hair that any other voice, any other ideas than hers, must not be mine, either.

I want you here too. I want you both. I want the Bull's body and its hair and sweat and the helplessness and friction and heat. Your love has been so long chaste, these six years, that I have just white-shaded memories to tell me of your human body moving with mine after dark. But you, my love, my black-haired blue-eyed heart, the other half of my whims and indulgences and insensibility, I want you on the pillow next to mine when I remake Amelia from the raw creature the Bull makes of me. An old unfaithfulness is this three-pointed star, but I find it no less a puzzle. Do we still understand each other? Seven years I've been in this city alone, selling my voice, navigating beds like islands floating on the river, and you still abed under the great tree, moldering, lingering.

Should you not seek a city of your own?

My grip loosens. I still do not know what I want, where to go, what pushes or pulls at me. But her light—these years, there has been no light. No beacon to follow. Her no-light has led me nowhere. I have crawled and walked and run without motion: no longer breaking down, yet immobile.

The Corisande that belonged to me was a girl as I was. Her book is written and ended. Mine is daily written and reopened. What does she have to give me?

The pillow is blank. *I'd do anything. Tell me what I should say to keep you here.* I did pull her, by the heel, by the eyes. I owe her the life she might have had. (These are habits, these thoughts.)

But it was not me who dropped out of the boat and crammed stones in her pockets. That was not me. That was my Corisande.

Dawn. I turn away from the dumb, senseless pillow, close my eyes. By and by, sleep arrives, and with it, oblivion.

VIII

One morning I wake and though Corisande is still gone, others have come. Whispering. *We are here.* The girls in the pews before Irma and me at the Baccalaureate.

They do not appear; they whisper. *We know you. We see you. You belong with us.*

I lie in bed and listen. Are they here for me, really? Or for Corisande? I have not seen anyone for two weeks (Miss Audra Rose is on her third honeymoon; someone [Malcolm] has called and called and I have not answered) and I do not know, in fact, if I'm alive or dead.

We see you.

I miss my love. Her and the idea of her and the object I've nursed for twelve years that I made out of her and stored in my heart. Never have I traveled straight into the Cartwright School built inside those chambers—I danced around it, or hovered over it, never venturing face-forward. True, it was my place and Corisande's, and I dreamed of the lake and roamed in the graveyard, eyes shut, and felt her hands on my skin, her hair on my fingertips. But the Directress's office, with the door closed. The rooms where a girl slept alone after the other bed emptied, no warning. The library and its vaults, airless, the stench of unread books and unmoved dust. These I did not see with open eyes.

You belong with us.

No. I can't go back. My life is here.

Your life is nowhere.

I don't miss you. I don't want to see you, any of you.

You are our daughter.

I am no one's daughter. No one's.

Ave Maria. Come home.

I try to say I don't have a home, either, but these missing elements of identity are too much, stacked as they are in reply, and my voice shrinks to a marble. Alone. No one's child, no one's sister, no one's tenant. Is it a bed of my own I lie in? How long before I'm found?

You are not lost.

Where is my Corisande? For the first time in a thousand days I want to know.

Come home.

◆ ◆ ◆

No one sings like me, they say, at the Labyrinth. They come and tell me this when I descend to the floor. I let them put their hands on me and then I follow the Bull. The bartendress tosses me a ball of string, some nights, and I unravel it around the bed to ward off devils. I make rings of it. It leads nowhere. I can still hear the band from there, the piano notes moving in a slow arc. What goes up the scale must come down again.

Lately they have been singing with me. Nothing of you—your bright blue eyes, once, only once, in someone else's face at the back of the crowd—but I hear them between the notes. They know Gershwin, too, I guess. A matter of time until I see them, too.

The Labyrinth is not home.

I repeat myself, again and again, night after night, sing and fuck and sleep and sing and fuck and sleep. The eternal return, perhaps. Years of it. They grow louder. I cannot ignore them forever.

Nothing appears to save me. No beacon to show me the way. I repeat myself. I repeat myself.

They whisper all around me. They live in the air of my apartment, between the threads of my pillowcases. In the molecules. In the wires. Under my hair.

Did you know this, too? Did you hear them, smell them, see them on the walls and windows of our very own room, before you stepped into the lake? Did they sing?

Or did you ever know this music? You never knew a man's

touch, a mother's love, the shudder of an accelerator under your instep. I mourn for what you missed. I think of you wistfully, these days: lost, that mind and heart, opportunities unrealized. It's me who lived. Me, beaconless. I don't understand.

I don't want to leave this place. The merest possibility that this is home.

◆ ◆ ◆

It may be a dream, may all be from then to now, maybe, but I call Cleo and convince her to lend her car indefinitely and I go indomitable across desert and meadow, across land and sea, but at the end of the road, instead of something, is nothing. The school is in ruins and the forest is razed and the lake is dry.

Or this is the truth in my heart, and when I travel I find instead that the Baccalaureate still sings today, that the Directress in her gray shroud still holds sway on the unfortunates in the empty pews, and the great curving oak guards you from harm and meddling well into the next century, after all of this should have been melted down and re-formed into bright plastic and hidden wires. The Cartwright School is eternal, and Amelia is the ruin.

Or that is the truth in my mind, and I never left my bed. They await me still. Cleo's car idles below in the street.

Come home, oh, come home. Chase it through the valves and valleys of your heart, the folds and furrows of your mind, chase home,

chase family, chase what lies behind you until you find the past on its
ground and all the paths through the forest decay to nothing around your
deathless heart. See what is real, under your fingers, through your pupils,
light striking the rods and cones and projecting the truth, as it exists in
the ephemeral now, directly on the tissues of your brain. Perception's
rot can follow, in its own perpetual chase, but in the meantime, for that
sliver of a life, you will have seen it.

Yes. I am going. Passing through genuine geography to bear witness to whatever bedevils my bed. Cleo's car idles. I descend the stairs, close the door on the whispers, the abject abjurations. All day I've been listening to them, and evening dims out the city's detail, makes it lovely on the edges and impenetrable in the middles. A band warms up at Oliver's, down the block, the pianist impatiently plunking C, C, C while the bassist twangs over and under. Someone must be selling lavender from a cart nearby, because the scent is a cool bath, lidding the brew of fish and piss and smoke and cigars that usually wafts up from the pavement. In place of contempt, the warmth of affection for this dank block of an indifferent city.

Your life is nowhere.

Really? Is that true? Bed to bed and the house of holograms that imprisons the Bull doesn't feel like a life, but this block doesn't feel like nowhere. I've begun adding furniture to my room, hanging things on the walls. Arrayed my clothes the way I liked them in the closet. Things I could touch, not the insensible mist of Corisande and her fleet of ghouls.

You belong with us.

HONK. A truck of lettuces that can't fit around Cleo's car, in which I sit and grip the wheel and gaze up at the dusked building where I hang my hats. It doesn't mean I can't try it, now that Corisande has fled. I could fashion something out of that closet, this street, the habits circling me, building like candy floss around a paper cone. Cardboard and glue. I need not stay a shadow. The ghost-girls would leave me, too, if I brought other voices inside my door.

But where am I going? What beacon?

HONK-HOOOOOOOOOOOOONK.

C-C-C-C-C. "Come on, Metz."

Come home.

In the last analysis, I can't say if I weakened, if my path was fated, if I found the old grounds easier to tread than the new, if I was called by something stronger than a will of my own. But in this twilight, I shift the gear and put my heel on the pedal and I drive toward the falling night, toward the curtain drawn over the whispers that reach for me.

IX

It was not I who called Amelia to return. No matter how I might have wanted her, wanted to yank her away from the tether of that *creature* who abducted her out of her bed, I did not ask her. The others decided it was nigh. The girls who once decided to lift me up.

It isn't always night here. But it isn't often day. Afternoons may be as hollow and silent as witching hours, though knotted with less myth and mystery. The stillness before teatime needs more boogeymen. Just as many ill sins may be clothed in those quiet hours as in the wee ones.

Amelia's path could be traced easily from where I laid. I lifted my hand and watched her travel the roads and lanes from wrist to thumb; she turned fingerward, and I followed her. Shadows gave chase, but she proved quick and carried her own darkness. I might have joined her in the passenger seat, could have slept in the back to comfort her, but the wound of the Bull still smarted. Beating hearts had more ichor than mine, but a Bull? I trembled for her, for the alien hands that gulped her flesh, the fearful strength of the limbs that entwined with hers. She did not know the forces she had invited into her body. She could not know, could not understand. I had a longer view.

What I saw varied, depending on my concentration. Under the oak tree, I saw the forest crumbling, new water flowing from the lake to the faraway sea, forming a river across the lawn where I lay, our stones chipping and eroding and washing away. Even against those harbingers of the far future I saw Amelia dancing with the evening breeze on the fresh earth over me. One era coupled with another; I saw girls in thick white dresses brushing the tips of their handmade boots, covered throats and bound braids, processing to the chapel; against them pressed girls with jagged bobs and bare knees, their rouge unremarkable; against them no one, no procession with fashions to critique, just the clunk of brick against brick as the chapel's mortar decayed. The school already vanished, shaded by lost trees. They moved the stones but not the bones beneath. Ever I stayed under the oak tree and saw the blend of centuries, frenzy and silence, and I waited for Amelia to come.

She journeyed unafraid. She even remembered the way. It shook me how old she seemed, how the years between the Amelia who cartwheeled in the grass and the Amelia who crossed land and sea to meet us comprised a realm I couldn't visit. Not really. I'd seen her through it all, but she had lived, and I hadn't, and I saw, anew, for what it was, that gravity pressing on her skin.

✦ ✦ ✦

Let me tell you how we came to love each other.

In the first class on the first day—trigonometry, at the absurd hour of seven-thirty in the morning—she sat behind me and looked at the stray hairs leaking from my braids. (Her curls always stayed where they were placed.) She'd never seen hair so black, against skin so white—she told me it looked like the night sky against a bleached bedsheet. She made a constellation out of the freckles on my neck, above the itchy lace collar my aunt had sent for me to wear on my first day. Amelia had thought the collar very pretty, so delicate, and I gave the dreadful thing to her to keep that very afternoon. She had told me she thought the collar meant I was a proper lady, a starched and upright girl who studied her lessons well and would go on to marry a town doctor. Oh my dearest.

We did not know then of our standing as roommates. When our classes ended at two-thirty we followed our separate ways back to the same room, and she glanced at my forehead and then gazed steadily at the floor until bedtime, nodding and shivering her head at my timid questions. The one glimpse of her hazel eyes lit up my skin, like neon illuminating the jukebox after a long, dozy afternoon in the drugstore. Something stalked, restive, behind those eyes, something that kept her foot beating a tattoo against her chair's leg as she read Dickens or D.H. Lawrence before dinner, something that turned her body like the ocean after lights-out.

She barely spoke to me for three days, though her voice, even at fourteen, was resonant and fascinating. She had so few clothes that I offered the loan of some of mine, and she pinned my skirts to her skinny waist with gratitude directed right at the floorboards, still. I couldn't give her shoes, or replace her grubby half-pencils, but I helped her with the lye soap the nurse pressed upon her for her lice. She squeezed her hazel eyes shut against the burn but emitted no sound. These were the secrets of her poverty. Such secrets were common at the orphanage, and Cartwright had a handful of orphanage girls like her—at least one for every year—but I kept them close, anyway, without her needing to ask. Her head bent so deeply with shame that she made a millstone of it. I had no business in removing that weight, even though I knew, as she did not, that a shame shared is a burden lifted.

On the third night she woke me with dreadful weeping cries. Half-gasps, half-shrieks, tears wetting her curls. I went to her bed and shook her awake. Like a tiny child she clung to me, heaving, too immersed in terror to remember her millstone.

"Never let me go," she whispered. Her fingers trembled as she clutched me, my sleeve, my hair. "Never let me go."

Had I known all, I might not have held her closer and

promised, no, never, darling, I'll never, but I did not know all and those promises passed my lips.

I stroked her back, like an infant, until she fell asleep.

The next morning she smiled at me, a smile like a wince but the first I'd had. I asked her a question about the trig teacher and she answered (something slanderous, I assume) and before I knew it we were in a genuine conversation. Tentative, awkward, bumpy as a farm road, but extant.

It took her all of the first term to bloom in toto: to eat without hoarding, to look classmates in the eye, to laugh without halting, to sing in the bathroom (and thus captivate everyone, like Orpheus, stilling the faucets and even the swinging door), to stop dreaming whatever woke us both and extracted the same promise from me night on night. Never let me go. Never let me go. I was easily in love with her from the first time she took my hand on the way back from dinner and swung it, listening while I chattered about vacant-headed Desdemona and why on earth our English teacher wept at Carol the Small's wholly mediocre recitation of the death scene. I didn't let on, I just wrapped my fingers lightly around Amelia's and protested Desdemona's self-destruction with hardly a pause. But she had won me, Amelia. Then and there.

I returned to my aunt's house for the winter holidays that year, while Amelia remained at Cartwright with the rest of the orphan girls. Something odd and fierce hunkered in her eyes as she bid me adieu. I wanted to kiss her but it seemed absurd to do it. Carol the Great talked about kissing boys—her cousin, just to try it out (both parties were unimpressed), and a boy at a cotillion once (his lips felt thick and dry, like a broad plant sitting in the sun). Why should a girl want to kiss a girl? Was that something that happened?

On the first night after I returned from my aunt's house—the little room encased in wood walls with no one's furniture and a worn Oriental rug—Amelia climbed into my bed and answered those questions. When I asked her, at an intermission, how she knew what to do, she said she learned from the girls at the orphanage. She silenced my other questions with kisses, sliding her fingers up, down, around, and inside, finding delicious places to inhabit, teaching me to spelunk for pleasure in the caves our bodies made among the rough bedsheets.

Lights-out showed me what I'd been knocking against for the whole first term: we were in love with each other. Sensible Corisande protested our ages, our sex, our situation, our wildly different personalities, but Amelia's unswerving hazel eyes towed me back to the sheltered cabin we shared in the Good Ship Cartwright. Her nightmares faltered, became fewer and farther between, and eventually stopped. I'd look up from Sappho and find her studying me; she'd cling to my hand to the last possible moment before we divided for separate classes. Never let me go.

The girls told us we were cute or said nothing; the teachers merely said nothing.

Three years passed.

When she returned from the summer holidays, that autumn we became sixth-form girls, Amelia's nightmares accompanied her. Nothing held them at bay. And I noticed odd things that term: voices in unpeopled hallways, movement in the empty pews the Directress set aside for the alumnae of Cartwright who had passed on, a chill in the sun-strewn library carrel I preferred. Darkness curtained the school at night, muffled it closely. Light came as through cheesecloth. The Directress kept catching my eye in the hall.

We made plans for the future, Amelia and I.

"We'll move to the city," I said.

"You'll go to college and I'll work," she said.

"I'll get my inheritance in three years," I said.

"We'll get a house on the coast," she said.

"I can swim in the ocean every day," I said.

"I'll learn to play the piano," she said.

"I want to be a professor like my father," I said.

"I just want to be with you," she said. "I don't care what I do with my days, I just want to sleep in the same bed as you."

Instructors pressed her on this last point, but her direction remained unfixed, floating, tethered only to me. Even this hardly fretted me, while all else weighed heavy. The path of a sparrow became an arc that described my life. The droning music of the chapel's organ brought me to tears. Everything, everything carried significance like a bundle tied to its back, because school was ending, my life was changing, and I knew not what lay ahead.

Amelia consulted the lines on my palm one night, playacting a thickly accented fortune-teller, and told me I loved water and would soon go on a long journey. I gazed at my hand by firelight after she'd fallen asleep, the roads and the clearings, the geography of what I clasped and held.

That night I was visited by a nightmare of my own. I sat in the empty pews of the chapel and watched while the Directress, robed in silken gray, sliced open the belly of a bleating lamb and picked through its viscera. My favorite teacher, Miss Finley, comforted the animal, which whined pitifully but refused to expire. "It is you," intoned the Directress, and pointed a bloody finger at me.

I stood up and left the chapel in no especial hurry. Once outside, thunder rolled through the forest and across the campus. Amelia screamed and beat on a window from a third-floor classroom in the building across the footpath from the chapel. The thunder continued, and as I turned to face the lake, I found that it was not thunder, but a river, loosed from a dam somewhere nearby, rushing closer in a great wave that could not but overtake me.

Amelia shrieked my name. I did not move. *It is me.*

The river crushed me where I stood, and I woke. That night, it was she who comforted me.

"Never let me go," I whispered. "Never let me go."

X

Had their lives been exchanged, Corisande would have found a way to forget her first love and shape a life that didn't take place only in beds and basements. She would have mourned and she would have let go. But that is not this story; it was not Amelia who perished. Our mistress's displeasure has drained us of color, of song, of scent. We can't change it, can't take it back, can't remove Corisande from our ranks. Some things even the Directress cannot do.

There are no straight lines at our Cartwright. All things meander from one point to the next, looping, arabesqueing, crisscrossing. No flat smooth stones, but surfaces softened and slumped by time. No horizon, but a jagged forest. No structure, but a myriad of buildings reimagined and knocked through by well-meaning architects, palimpsests visible only to us. To us and the Directress.

Along the shapely road she came, the same soft edges and curving lines under her tires and under her hair, hot with purpose, back back back to her Corisande who sleeps beneath the great oak. Who fled to us when the Bull interfered. His season of rapacity short in myth, but long in memory. Poor dear Corisande. And Amelia comes to waken her, to bind her here again. We sing to ourselves, Ave Maria, trying to see the way.

We have been here since the Greeks built their temples, and we have been here since last night's stroke of twelve. We will be here only through tonight's bell tolling, and we will be here until Amelia's city is as ruined as the Coliseum. It is never and always the Baccalaureate where we appeared and tried to lift our sister out of this place.

Colorless. Once we wore blue, our whispers noisy enough to startle deer nosing around the stones. We will wear black, to bid farewell, but that is soon and not soon. (This isn't easy.) When Amelia comes, in her car, we wear white, our skin flushless, our eyes rinsed with glacier meltwater, cold and clear.

The Directress stirs, when the motor shuts off, her summer slumber troubled by an ill dream. Amelia pauses with one heeled shoe on the macadam, half out the car door, her dress umber, a veiled hat on her curls, scanning the peaked roofs. The backs of her legs sweat quietly. She thinks *forgiveness*. She thinks *Never let me go*. She thinks some other things that we do not know, about the city and the Bull. She has songs of her own that we could not learn.

Alleluia. Gratia plena.

She removes her shoes. Unrolls her stockings and pitches them in the open car window. Leaves on the hat, the veil obscuring her vision with small netted squares. Her stride does not fool us. But she does remember the way.

Our ranks swell each year, girls who come at the Directress's bidding and remain after the families find the rest and take them away. Girls who are not missed, who were never not lost and are now fallen through the last crack. Sometimes the end of the tether to their bodies is a mere relief, because their bodies were used only to torture them. These do not want the next phase, the lifting light at the Baccalaureate. They want to sing here, to know what they had been denied. We all sing together.

Except Corisande. She is the only one who refused the light altogether. She doesn't have to sing. She can speak, even if it's only to Amelia.

Daylight still waxes, or at least it does for Amelia. She must be hungry. (Some of us have been here so long that we miss food, hovering in the rafters while the real girls eat, watching their indifferent sipping and chewing.) She steps upon the grass. *Concentrate*, she thinks. *You have been unfaithful*, she thinks.

We sing quieter. The Directress drifts off on our melody.

Corisande rises up. The stones still drag her pockets open, her hair still drips. Her eyes, though, bright blue. The first color we have seen under the great oak since we ourselves wore dresses of the same hue.

"I'm sorry," says Amelia. She thinks something else, but unformed, beyond our horizon. And Corisande would dazzle her eyes, but for the veil.

"Come here," says Corisande. "Come back to me."

Amelia's thought clears, but not enough, and she moves closer to the headstone.

"I love you," says Corisande.

"I know." We all know. Minor key, now, altos *forte*.

"Come back." A whisper.

"I did," says Amelia. She tears off her hat. "I am."

They tangle together at last, under the great oak, the quick and the dead in the harmony that we form. Like bedclothes tenting, softening sin. They whisper to each other, *Amelia, Corisande*, and each whisper brightens our song. A mist over Cartwright lifts. *Corisande. Amelia*. The trees burst into fall, umber as her discarded dress, red as her beating heart. The lake laps blue. The grass verdant, breathing. *Amelia, Corisande*. The Directress stirs, but we sing *fortissimo*, plucking the luminous strings of our hair, the fear struck out of us by enchantment. Every color shivers with excitement. Our eyes illuminate green, hazel, blue, violet. Our dresses slathered with life.

Corisande. Amelia. Their love is raucous and fearless under the tree. They cleave and re-merge in a sheaf of time that we cannot observe. Twilight falls, an opal spreading its fiery heart across the firmament, shading to deeper and deeper sapphires. The nightingales emerge. We turn to lullaby. Amelia breathes on her back.

She thinks *Goodbye.* We hiccup on a grace note.

"What do you mean?"

"This is the last thing I can give you," says Amelia. "I don't want ghosts around me anymore. I want to forget this place."

We turn from lullaby to lament.

"You can't," says Corisande.

"You jumped out of the boat!" Amelia cries. "You left me. You left me alone. No one ever loved me until you."

"I still love you now."

"There is no you. There is no Corisande. She's dead. You're not real, you're no more real than the bull horns I kept seeing on Malcolm. I have to live in the real world."

"Malcolm's bull horns are real," says Corisande.

"No! No. I've had enough. I've hidden for too long. I'm going to sing. My voice, my face. No more shadow."

The Directress is full awake and listening, rigid in her berth.

"You can't leave me."

Amelia zips up her dress. "Yes, I can."

"I made a bargain," says Corisande. "I made a trade."

The Directress bolts out of bed. Our lament darkens.

"I don't know anything about that." She adjusts her hat.

"You're the orphan. I was supposed to go home after the Baccalaureate. Not you."

"You're an orphan, too," says Amelia. She thinks what. what.

"I have my aunt. You don't have anybody."

This stops her, for a moment. What. But then she blinks. Blinking is semi-autonomic, in that Amelia's brain may send a message to the muscles around Amelia's eyes telling them to cause a blink without her explicit permission; but she can also blink at her choosing. The physiology of this motion, of the blink and of her noticing it, reminds her that she is alive. She is alive, and Corisande is not. Whatever family each of them had, until the night before Baccalaureate, until Corisande leapt into the lake and placed stones in her pockets (for whatever reason she did this), is irrelevant. She is alive. She blinks again. She is alive.

"I'm telling you I want a family," she says. "I want friends. Not ghosts, not shadows, not a creepy school no one's heard of. Real people, a real home, a real life."

The Directress halts at her door, buttoning her collar.

"I love you. But I'm not coming back." Tears drip from her chin but her voice has no weak spots, no holes. "I don't know what will happen but I'm not coming back."

The lament softens, slows.

Corisande sags, the dark crown of her head a smear above

her gravestone. "But I traded," she says. "I traded for you."

Amelia is already gone, already half out of the cemetery. *I can't leave without her*, she thinks. *I can't live without her.* She gets into her car and fits her pumps on her feet. *I can't leave this place. I can't make a home by myself.* She starts the car.

"You're singing at the Labyrinth tonight," she mutters. And leaves. Again, and always.

XI

I sing at the Labyrinth. I sidle away from Malcolm and his hot breath on my neck. I sleep quietly, no dreams. I take walks in the late mornings to keep the sun nearby.

One month.

I sing at a club called Tip of the Tongue, one molasses Wednesday, as a tryout. They want me. I quit the Labyrinth with a letter on the bar. I don't return Malcolm's calls, or Cleo's. Tip of the Tongue has a normal stage with a band and a spotlight, me in a cocktail dress, a real back door. No sleepy blond youths, no secret passages, no mirages behind the bar.

Two months.

I advertise as a typist. A writer named B. Wasserman hires me by mail. I type B. Wasserman's closely written notebook pages on my Olivetti and mail them back. B. Wasserman hires me again. The writing is full of swords and maidens. Silly stuff, nothing that I'd read for my own pleasure.

Three months.

A vine of heliotrope climbs over my balcony. I think of her, of Corisande, for the first time since. She never saw heliotrope, though she loved the word. I miss her, but it's a school friend I miss. The greatest infatuation of those feverish years. How could I have been so careless? We might have been caught and punished. Tip of the Tongue bristles with horror stories. Persecution. Loss.

Four months.

B. Wasserman must have spoken well of me. I type so busily now that my below-neighbor complains. I save up enough to move, leave behind Malcolm's scent (clinging to the bedsheets) and voice (murmuring under every telephone call). But the heliotrope blooms so prettily.

Five months.

I sing "My Man" without a catch in the low notes. But I keep my eyes closed the whole way, closed or lowered to the pedals of the piano, worked by Sid's brown wing-tip. After, three men and one woman buy me drinks. None of them is right. None of them guessed what I wanted in my glass.

Six months.

Turning the paperback rack at Woolworth's and there is B. Wasserman. Something called *In the Clutches of the Dead*. The title startles me enough to spend a quarter. (I did not type this book.) Two days later, I reread B. Wasserman's biography again and again, until I have its miserly words as well memorized as any of Mlle. Poirier's French lessons:

The author of half a dozen Pocket titles, B. Wasserman was born and raised in Chicago. He lives with his family in the northeast, but dreams always of Camelot.

Foolish. Meaningless. Just as my hunch that the cramped half-moons and spikes of B.'s writing drew a woman's hand on the page. But *In the Clutches*...I think of the heroine Lucia, of the green hill she died on, for many days before I think of Corisande again.

Seven months.

Restless, I push aside my nightgown. I think of Malcolm with Corisande's face. Of his pressure with her hands on me. Monstrosify the monster and the maiden. I peak and I cry and I read B. Wasserman's biography again. *Dreams always of Camelot.* What a simpleton. I am no maiden. No heroine.

Eight months.

I type very bad articles bound for academic journals. "Mr. Faulkner and the Demon Drink." "Nevermore, Opium: The Poppy in Poe." "P.B. Shelley's *Frankenstein*: The Myth and the Truth." B. Wasserman keeps poor company. Female-haters and temperance fiends. I owe him this patronage, I think, I believe, because the advertisement for my services stopped appearing months ago, and these dreadful articles keep pouring in. I stop singing "My Man" altogether and add "Let's Face the Music and Dance." Irving Berlin, again, half minor and half major.

Nine months.

One of the books I typed for B. Wasserman appears in the paperback rack at Woolworth's. No author photo. The words "with his family" have been excised from his biography. I haven't seen his handwriting in three months. Neither has Malcolm found the new flat I rented a few streets south of where I was. He has not called, nor do I smell him in the bedsheets, nor do I see his steamy breath on my window in the morning. I dream of Corisande, but her face is smeared. Blue and black over a white dress. I miss her in concept but not in ghostflesh. There is no heliotrope on my balcony, so I've bought a little cactus to take care of, instead.

Ten months.

I go out with Sid once or twice just to be presentable. He has beautiful hands, dancing fingers, not meaty and cavernous like Malcolm's. He loses interest in my words even as he listens to my voice. I see nothing in him, behind him, no equivalent to the years I spent at Cartwright, the years I spent alone. With a ghost. He kisses me on the cheek. I smile with my lips. I can smell the cold, Sid's nervous cologne, my hair. I say thank you.

Eleven months.

At last, a parcel from B. Wasserman. He encloses some pages for me to type. A note at the top: "This may be a little different." It is. The maiden is *angry*. She stomps through her tale furiously. She is punished. She pays the punishment back a thousandfold.

She burns the bridge she has trodden out of her own kingdom, and that is all B. Wasserman has sent me: the origin of the fury-maiden's journey.

She confuses me. Where does her anger go? Where does it come from? What lies beneath it, beyond it? Doesn't her fire burn out without consuming anything but itself, like a bit of flashpaper? Are maidens allowed to be angry? Are they allowed to show it? Can they still be loved?

Corisande never got angry. The Directress never got angry. I got angry a few times, but I felt worse, not better. Irma got angry a lot but her roommate used to pour cups of water over her head if she lost her temper, so she learned.

Sid asks me to sing "Baby, It's Cold Outside" together, and I say no. I sing "I'll Be Seeing You" and "Get Thee Behind Me, Satan" and "You Are My Lucky Star." I like torch less and less, and Gershwin more and more.

Finally I type a letter to put in with the pages. *Sir, I don't know you, but the tenor of this new book disturbs me greatly. You know the business of writing books better than I, but I know the business of being female better than you, and I find Candice, your character, difficult to comprehend. If she is based on someone you know, or knew, I apologize for my presumption. But if she is a whole invention, I wonder if she needs more circumspection before she is presented to the reading public.*

Not wise of me to throw away B. Wasserman's sponsorship.

But the compulsion to speak my mind is irresistible.

Twelve months.

A letter arrives from B. Wasserman. *Madam, I don't know you, but your letter gave me food for thought so unpalatable that I chewed it like cud. I would like to meet you. Is this possible? I live in your city and can visit a public location of your choosing. Please reply promptly.*

No, it is not possible. My life has settled, at last, the oil and water separating like reasonable elements, no bad dreams, no Bull, no desperation for what I've missed or am missing. I begin to feel motion. My no-light beacon is behind me.

B. Wasserman is a man who wants to lecture. He wants time that belongs to me.

But I don't understand Candice. I want her answers. He is the only one who knows her. That throws us together.

And so one morning (a Wednesday in July, wet heat gleaming on every nose and forehead, the smell of deodorant working slavishly, dogs panting and too warm to pet), I take the subway down, down, into the mythmap of this city, the grid from which commerce and art steam off like evaporating sweat. I go to a diner B. Wasserman has named. I order coffee. I wait.

A woman enters the diner as if she carries no weight, as if nothing has ever bowed her back. The diner is not a diner, but a court, of law or of antiquity, and she is unafraid of a single person. She has Corisande's eyes.

This last is not unusual. I see Corisande's eyes on myriad strangers, on record albums, in paintings and films. But in this face the eyes do not belong to Corisande. Her eyes are like a melody transposed and woven into a new song, until you can strain and hear the old tune, but the new song is so natural that it sounds as though it was written that way. Eventually, the old melody vanishes from its silent context, is no longer isolated from the home it's found. And then there is just a song.

The woman hesitates at my table. "Are you Amelia?"

"Yes," I say. Is she B. Wasserman's assistant? His wife?

"I'm Beatrice Wasserman," she says. "Thank you for coming to meet me."

Oh. I am not the only one with secrets.

She slides in across from me. Her smile is the way in: it isn't regal and assured, like the rest of her. It trembles at the edges. Unused muscles, or high nerves.

"I'm sorry for what I wrote to you," I say. "I wouldn't have been…I didn't know."

"That is the point of an alias," she says. She fans her face with both hands, limply.

"Anyway, I'm sorry."

"Iced tea, please," she says to the waitress, who has been standing near the table long enough for me not to notice her anymore. "And a dish of whipped cream."

The waitress's gum drops into her cheek. "Just whipped cream?"

"Yes."

"No pie or ice cream or nothing?"

"Just the whipped cream," says B. Wasserman.

"All right," says the waitress, as if she has been asked for a bowl of live snapping turtles, and walks off without asking me if I want anything.

"You didn't want to meet me just to tell me off, did you?" I ask.

"No," she says. Corisande's eyes look at my hands, wrapped around my water glass. My fingers are a little numb, even as the backs of my knees sweat. Heat leaks from the kitchen, the door, the scattered patrons. "I wanted to thank you."

"Thank me?"

The whipped cream arrives and B. Wasserman scoops a pile of it into her mouth with a spoon. "Mmmm," she says. "Cool."

I would never have thought of this, but it looks lovely.

"It's so hot," she says. Her hair, an unremarkable ash brown, has been gathered into a braided bun at the crown of her head. The braids shine with moisture. The style is stern, at first glance, but it denotes effort and some little vanity. I could have told her that her eyes deserved a little more care and her hair a little less, but she is not my business.

"Thank me?" I say again, to her closed eyes. She has tipped her head back, moving her jaws gently to swoosh the whipped cream around.

"You made me think," she says to the ceiling. "Mmm. Not so many typists make me think."

"You said it was unpalatable, what I said."

She pins me with your eyes. Dizzying. "I do not understand a woman who does not understand rage."

I think of the Bull. Of the skin that barely contained him, of the reddened raised scratches I'd find on my body. Madam, I'm Malcolm. "I understand rage," I say. "I don't think it's realistic in a female character."

She laughs, and that is a little like Corisande too. People turn to look. She doesn't cover her mouth or snitter through her nose. Like the bun, it lifts her veneer, or lightens it. Or mars it. "Come and see me during my monthlies," she says. "You'll find it plenty realistic."

I don't laugh, and she appears subdued for the first time.

"What kind of life is it that has never known rage?" she asks, looking right at me now, not fussing with what's on the table.

"I've known rage."

"But not in a woman."

"I never knew my mother," I say. "The nuns were cruel, but always patient. A woman never lost her temper in front of me, or because of me."

A beat, or a clock-tick. "Whom have you loved?"

"You were talking about rage."

"And now I'm talking about love. They press against each other like lovers on either side of glass. They are eye to eye."

I shake my head. Her words are more arresting even than yours. (She is a writer.) My heart is timpani in my ears. "No."

"I'm afraid so, Amelia," she says. My name is a vine of flowers uncurling in her mouth.

"I have loved," I say. I bite my lip too hard and blood collects under my tongue. I don't know how we got here. I have, I have, I want to cry. I have so.

"Tell me," says B. Wasserman, and your eyes bite into me. I am delicious in her mouth, and there's only blood in mine, so I take a spoonful of her whipped cream without asking. The clouds of it mingle with salt and copper. *Tell me. Tell me. Tell me.* She means it. She would not kid about love, I think.

So I tell her your story. I tell her about my Corisande, about the lake and the white dress and the Ave Maria and the Directress's gray eyes. I tell her about seeing my Corisande again, one year ago, and about the upward slant of my situation since then. I do not tell her about the Bull. Either she already knows of him, learned of him in the original Greek and has written his story as a Woolworth's paperback, or she would not believe me. I think she already knows.

When I'm finished telling, the lunch crowd has thinned to a few old-timers ruffling newspapers and tapping their mugs for more coffee. B. Wasserman has eaten all of her whipped cream and drunk two glasses of iced tea without taking your eyes off me. The waitresses are smoking and nattering behind the counter, not even bothering with us.

"I'd like to write about her," says B. Wasserman. "About Corisande. Would you let me do that? Would you help? Collaborate with me, I mean?"

What? "What about the Candice book?"

She knots her hands together. "I think I was wrong about Candice," she says. "If you can't make sense of Candice, maybe it's not time for her yet. I'd rather write about Corisande."

"I want you to," I whisper, before I can stop my mouth.

"Let's strike a bargain," says B. Wasserman. "I'll write, you type. And correct me if I get anything wrong. Whatever I'm paid for the book, fifty percent is yours. Royalties and all."

So many buts. What if we don't like each other. What if you tell it wrong and I can't change your mind. What if no one wants the book. What if Corisande finds us both, and what if her rage does exist. The only one I can speak is "What about your family? Shouldn't they have a say in who gets your royalties?"

"What family?" She digs through her purse and extracts a

fountain pen. "You mean the biography?" She shakes the pen. "Oh, it's not true. Belongs to Barry, not Bea. Aha." She has located a tiny memo pad with a black leather cover. "I'll put it in writing."

"Barry?"

"Barry Wasserman. He's the pseudonym. I dreamed up a whole life for him. He's not much like me, though his writing is similar." She laughs again, and it sounds not like you but like her. I am beginning to know her.

"I don't…I don't know."

She scribbles on the pad. "It's all right if it doesn't work. But I know a good story when I hear one. I'm not letting Corisande's get away." She holds the pen out, cap first. "Let's put it on paper."

I read the scribble. It seems fair. I listen for Corisande, or for the ghost-girls, or for someone to tell me no, don't, she doesn't care for you, you're a fool. Shut yourself back up and stop looking in her eyes.

No sound. Just the common shout of my heart, just B. Wasserman breathing, just the soft rattle of the diner's noise floating low above the linoleum.

I sign.

And then everything is different.

XII

There is no line between the future and the present. It's the ocean washing the land: the water reaches here, then here, then here. The sand's texture explains the tide. Shows where we are in the day, the month. The moon's gracious circles drawn in sloppy liquid lines, drying under the sun.

When I see her with the writer, I see those lines changing, the tide moving in and out. I see the writer teaching her to play the piano. I see them arguing in the kitchen, the writer shattering a whole stack of blue and white plates. I see the writer speaking in a classroom while she listens. I see them lying together on a sofa, reading.

I see them in the bed they share.

It's not a hovering over. It's not a stable position from which I spy. It's just being there. My presence is an element of the room, like the floor joists, like the scent of pinewood.

Between them they make lightning.

Music calls me beyond them. Singing. I find Cartwright, and either I dream of it in overlaid pages, or its possibilities are not fully settled. I see it forgotten, overgrown, a series of shipwrecked structures in a green sea. I see it bustling, with new buildings and new leadership. I see it crawling and covered with figures like silverfish, white eaters of bookstuff, quick and lithe, flashing with the colored eyes of children. I see the Directress looming, and I see her shadow, and I see no evidence that she ever existed.

But the music calls me.

I miss her, but it's not the same Amelia I see with the writer. All that floated and sloshed in her has calmed and settled. She laughs, and is thoughtful, and sighs her pleasure—all of these to her own will rather than seeking me (or the Bull) as an arbiter. The writer can't, doesn't, do that for her, so she must do it for herself.

Her obsession was not all that I loved. Not all.

They sing for me.

The past, too, is slippery. Here, as it moves before me, I capitulate to its colors and textures, but nothing is how I remember it. As if what I see is someone else's story of me, and Corisande is not a real creature. As if she is a whole invention, forgotten further and further each moment, and what lingers here on the sand is the memory.

The earth moves. The tide turns. The light fades, and a thousand thousand living things surrender the capsules of flesh that carried them.

I want her to see me again. I want her to *see* me, not to let that goodbye beneath the great oak, that summer, be the last time she feels my heart.

I had thought that we'd see each other again, after, whether I stayed here or ascended. I had thought she wanted that. But now there is the writer, and her new laughter.

They *sing* and *sing*.

If it had been the Bull, I might have stayed here. To change her mind, or to warn him away. But she never sees him again.

I want her to see me again. For one bright moment. I want her years to fall from her face.

Today she bought some groceries and carried them in her arms down the street to the apartment she shares with the writer. Sunny out today. She hummed. She smiled at a mewing window-cat. She did not see me. The tune she hummed was "Route 66." She has forgotten my music.

Their song says it's time for me to leave. She has seen enough of me. We are neither of us alone. I don't want to sink under the waves, and I don't want her to drown with me.

The tide is going out.

The Directress's gray eyes pierce me from the lighthouse, there on the other side of the channel. The undertow will drag me out again, but I will not need to breathe this time. Will not need a rescuer.

You are not my Corisande.

She sets to making dinner. Chops parsley. Pops a cherry tomato in her mouth. The writer has the door closed; behind it, she dances with language, pairs truths in a tango.

You are not my Corisande.

Sing me to sleep. Sing me to the other shore.

Here are the scissors. There is the moon.

Come home, Corisande. Come to higher ground. The bright moment is here.

She looks in the mirror above the dining table and she sees me. Her breath stops. She clasps her hands across her beating heart. She has grown old, I see, her hair gray and her eyes netted with decades of smiles, but she knows me. She knows the creature and the memory, all of me.

It was not too long to wait.

My Corisande.

Concentrate. Concentrate.

Concentrate.

My gratitude to:

Marissa Korbel. Julie Greicius. Christopher Higgs. Gloria Harrison. Jesse Clemens. Julie Pecoraro.

Katharine Haake. Lidia Yuknavitch. The Ojai Tribe.

Jesi Buell.

Mariana Magaña. I feel lucky that your art found me.

Everyone who answered permissions questions: Angelica Lopez-Torres, Megan Rickborn, Erin Dickerson, and Amy Weller.

Gayle Brandeis, Joanna C. Valente, Lidia again, duncan b. barlow.

Olivia Taylor Smith. Alyson Sinclair. Neal Pollack. Numerous editors, especially Tobias Carroll and Marisa Siegel. If I wrote more than one review for you, add yourself to this list.

Twitter. All the fellow writers who have encouraged me, told me they're excited about my work, or shared writing of mine on social media. This list is too long to make, which means I'm supremely blessed.

Matt above all.